First published October 2013

Candid Creation Publishing books are available through most major bookstores in Singapore. For bulk order of our books at special quantity discounts, please email us at enquiry@candidcreation.com.

AMANDA ANNANDA AND THE LIBRARY BOOK BOX

Author   : Alison Siemon
Publisher   : Phoon Kok Hwa
Illustrator : Lim-Anling
Editor   : Kwee Cheng
Layout   : Corrine Teng
Published by : Candid Creation Publishing LLP
               167 Jalan Bukit Merah,
               Connection One Tower 4, #05-12,
               Singapore 150167
Website   : www.SingaporeBookPublisher.com
Email   : enquiry@SingaporeBookPublisher.com
ISBN   : 978-981-07-6257-5

 Facebook/CandidCreationPublishing

National Library Board, Singapore Cataloguing-in-Publication Data
Siemon, Alison, 1969-
Amanda Annanda and the library book box / Alison Siemon. – Singapore : Candid Creation Publishing LLP, 2013.
pages cm
ISBN : 978-981-07-6257-5 (paperback)

1. Girls – Juvenile fiction. 2. Libraries – Juvenile fiction. I. Title.

PZ7
828.99343 -- dc23   OCN859376912

Amanda Annanda and the Library Book Box

Alison Siemon

Illustrated by Lim An-ling

Candid Creation Publishing

CHAPTER 1

The kids at school thought Amanda Annanda had a funny name, and they giggled every time the teacher called it out in class.

They made jokes, knowing that Amanda could hear everything they said.

"It should be Amanda Bandanna."

"No, Amanda Banana."

"I've got it – Amanda Salamander!"

Then they would burst into peals of laughter. This happened every day.

Amanda would sit there and feel very small. So small that she would scrunch up her body, and squeeze in as close as possible to her desk. When she was really scrunched up, her face would scrunch up as well. Once, one of her classmates told her that she looked ugly when she did that, and Amanda stuck out her tongue and said, "I hate you."

At the end of each day Amanda made the long walk home. Her classmates waved from the back seats of their parents' cars, and Douglas Dunkin, who everyone called Dougie, pulled faces at her whenever he went by. Until the day that Amanda pulled a face back at him.

No one ever asked her if she wanted a lift home, so she just put her head down and ignored them all. After half an hour of trudging down the same old road she was back home – to the sound of a screaming baby.

Her little brother was just learning to talk, but he already knew how to pull her hair if he got the chance.

She threw her school bag down on the floor.

"How was your day, dear?" asked Mum, with the baby over her shoulder.

"Same as usual."

"That's good, dear. Come and have your afternoon tea."

Amanda sat at the dining room table and munched and crunched on something yummy that Mum had made. Sometimes she got Anzac biscuits or chocolate slice. Today it was crackers with vegemite, and she always finished afternoon tea with a cold glass of milk.

Thank goodness Mum's a good cook, she thought.

This was actually one of Amanda's favourite times of the day, when Mum and the baby sat at the table with her. It was at these times she wished she could talk about school, but Mum was always fussing over the baby, and only pretended to listen.

"I'm going to do my homework," said Amanda, as she jumped off her chair and carried her dishes to the kitchen sink.

"That's a good girl. I'll call you when dinner's ready," said Mum, turning back to the baby again, smiling and making all those yucky goo-goo, ga-ga noises that didn't make any sense at all.

Amanda dragged her school bag by its straps along the corridor floor. She liked the scraping sound it made. When she got to her room she banged the door shut and flopped down on her bed. The baby started crying, and she tried to shut out its noise.

"Boring, boring, boring baby," she said darkly, then feeling that was being a bit mean, she unzipped her school bag and took out her homework.

Today there were a lot of maths problems to solve. Amanda hated maths. No wonder they were called problems! She sighed and pulled out her pencil case, and started her homework. She knew she was allowed to start reading her latest library book once everything was finished, so she tried to do things as fast as possible.

Amanda really loved reading. She loved reading so much that she went to the school library nearly every day to borrow new books. When her homework was finished she grabbed the books out of her school bag, and with a quiver in her heart, laid them on her lap. It was a bit like a ritual. She breathed in deeply and looked carefully at the front covers. Then she chose which one to read first.

Amanda had discovered the secret of books. She found out that when she read, she could forget the everyday stuff around her. She could forget the taunts, the teasing, and the sneering faces of the kids at school. She could forget being left out of games. She could even forget a bad mark on a test!

It was like magic when she opened a book. She never knew where the story was going to take her, and into what world she'd magically disappear.

4

Today's book was a collection of stories about goblins and witches. It seemed a little scarier than the princess book she'd read the day before.

I wonder what a goblin is? Amanda thought, and she started reading. The sunlight seemed to dim, and the walls of her room drew closer, until she felt like she was surrounded by stones of a dungeon wall.

She'd finished three stories when she heard Dad arrive home.

"I'm back!" he sang out.

"Well, that's obvious," said Amanda to herself, rolling her eyes. She read on, half-listening. She heard Dad go and talk to Mum. There were a few distant mutterings, followed by the sound of footsteps coming down the corridor.

BOOM, BOOM, BOOM!!!

Dad knocked on her dungeon door.

"How's my Princess?" he asked, his voice muffled by the wood.

"Go away!" yelled back Amanda – she still wanted to read.

"What? You don't want to see your poor old Dad?"

"Always interrupting, " Amanda grumbled, getting up reluctantly and opening the door to her cell.

"Hello, poor old Dad," she said.

5

"Thanks a lot," said Dad and he gave her a big hug. "What are you doing?"

"Reading."

"Oh. Trees? Bugs?"

"Goblins. And witches that cook up your bones!!!"

"Ugh…" said Dad. "I think we've got bones in our dinner tonight! I don't know whose they are. Are you ready to eat?"

With a nod and a laugh Amanda turned on her bedroom light for a second to check her room, and then grabbed Dad's hand. In the darkness of the corridor, it seemed as though a goblin or witch could jump out of the wall at any time!

She smiled up at him, and at the same time, Dad looked down and smiled back. *My Dad's all right, sometimes*, she thought.

They walked closer to the smells of wonderful cooking, and the friendly light of the dining room. Mum and the baby were already seated and there were plates of food on the table. Mum gave Amanda a big smile, the baby smiled too, and she began to feel a little better about things.

And that's what nearly every day was like, and she desperately wanted something to change.

CHAPTER 2

It was lunchtime at school. Kids were running around everywhere, climbing trees, playing tag, and dancing to the latest pop songs. Amanda was on her way to the library when suddenly a dark shadow fell across her path. It was Big Mel. Big Mel was the tallest kid at school, and she loved to torment and push other kids around.

"Hello, Skinnylegs," Big Mel smirked, and Amanda suddenly wished herself invisible. Everyone knew that if Big Mel talked to you, trouble would soon follow. "Where're you off ta?!"

"The library," mumbled Amanda.

"*The library,*" Big Mel mimicked, and out of nowhere her little troll friends appeared. They watched and giggled at all this cleverness. Amanda tried to move past them but Big Mel immediately grabbed her by the wrist.

"Let me go!" Amanda cried.

"Why should I?" said Big Mel, with a glint in her eye.

"LET ME GO!" Amanda yelled as loudly as she could.

Big Mel was twisting her arm so hard that she could feel the tears starting to sting her eyes.

"Cry baby, cry baby, look at the cry baby," sang Big Mel the Monster, now gnashing her teeth in anticipation.

She's going to eat me, thought Amanda, wincing in pain. Suddenly, out of the corner of her eye she saw Mrs Macintosh striding towards them with a furious face. Dougie Dunkin was running alongside, talking and pointing frantically at the small group.

Before Big Mel realised what was happening, her troll friends had scattered and she was caught out with her hand still tight around Amanda's wrist.

Mrs Macintosh's voice boomed out as she marched towards them.

"MELANIE MOORE, what do you think you're doing?"

Big Mel dropped Amanda's arm like a hot potato and turned to run, but Dougie reached them just in time and stuck his foot out in front of her. Big Mel tripped over it and went sprawling onto the concrete floor.

Mrs Macintosh bent down, puffing hard, and pretended not to see what had happened. She grabbed Big Mel by the back of her school jumper.

"You come with me, young lady," she snorted furiously, steam coming out of her ears.

With more strong words continuously flowing out of her mouth, she hauled Big Mel off to the Principal's office.

Dougie and Amanda were left standing there.

Amanda looked at Dougie awkwardly.

"Thanks for that, Douglas," she finally muttered, blushing.

"That's all right. She's so mean. She got little Gerty Small the other day, and no-one found out until it was too late," said Dougie.

Amanda looked at him in surprise. *He's brave*, she thought. And she'd never seen him look so angry. Dougie looked back at her, and Amanda blushed again and mumbled, "Thanks, again," before running off.

The bell rang as she made her way back to class, but Amanda had a big smile on her face. Something had just changed. Someone had just helped her. And maybe she had made a new friend – a boy friend. It didn't really matter what had just happened, she was just glad that Dougie had been there. She sat down at her desk, and forgot all about her lucky escape as the latest test was handed out.

CHAPTER 3

A few days later, Amanda was sitting on the floor of the library trying to decide which books she wanted to borrow. She had taken quite a few books off the shelf already, and was slowly browsing through them. It was difficult to decide what to read, because she could only borrow three books at a time, and there were hundreds of books to choose from.

She stood up and reluctantly put a collection of *Tales from the Far East* back on the shelf. Just as she was pulling her hand back someone tapped her on her shoulder and she jumped!

"It's okay. It's just me."

It was Dougie, smiling at her.

"Hello, Douglas," she said.

"What are you reading?" he asked.

"Nothing much," said Amanda.

There was a funny silence, then Amanda confessed, "It's difficult to choose."

Again, silence.

Amanda forced herself to say something else.

"What kind of books do you like?" she blurted out.

Dougie stopped and thought about it.

"Well, space stories and dragon stories are okay, but I like real adventure stories," he said.

"What do you mean 'real'?"

"Ones that could happen to anyone."

She looked at him quizzically.

He continued, "I mean, I don't think I'll ever be in space, so I don't really like science fiction, or that I'll ever meet a dragon – so that cuts out fairytales."

They looked at each other and laughed.

Amanda picked up three books from the pile beside her and then put the others back on the shelf where they belonged.

"Just hang on a second, I have to go and get these out."

She walked towards the librarian's desk and Dougie followed.

Mrs Pritchard was on duty.

"Oh, no," sighed Amanda to Dougie. "She's the mean one."

"Shhh!" said Dougie.

The thin lady rose stiffly from behind the desk. She peered down at Amanda over the glasses that precariously perched on her long, pointed nose.

"Yes girl?" Her voice screeched like chalk on a blackboard. "What do you want?"

"Could I please take these out, please?" Amanda said nervously.

"You don't need to say 'please' twice, girl!"

"Sorry."

Amanda bowed her head as the librarian grimaced and took hold of the books. As she turned away, Amanda sneaked another look at her. Mrs Pritchard always had her hair tied up in a bun. Amanda had heard it called a 'severe' bun once, by one of the mothers, but she hadn't yet worked out what that meant. Anyway, right now she just wished that jolly Mrs Bloom was there. Mrs Bloom always smelled of flowers and loved books just as much as Amanda did, and they always had something to talk about.

Her thoughts drifted sideways until she was yanked back into reality by two yellow eyes that came closer and closer towards her, floating over the big, wooden desk.

"Listen to me, girl. You can't borrow these books until you have returned the last ones," said Mrs Pritchard.

"I have returned them," said Amanda, in shock.

"Don't answer back!" said the librarian.

"But I did return them! I returned them this morning," Amanda declared loudly.

"Impertinence!" screeched Mrs Pritchard, and Amanda reminded herself to look up that word in the dictionary when she got home.

"Mrs Pritchard," she said levelly, "I put both the books back in the library book box before school this morning."

The librarian looked at her with a mixture of disbelief and rising anger.

"I'll go and check the box now," said Amanda quickly.

"I'll check with you," said Dougie, who had been silently shaking beside her.

They both rushed towards the big, wooden box just outside the library door. It was half-filled with books, and Amanda had to bend over to look inside.

"Can you see anything?" asked Dougie.

"Douglas! I've only just started looking!"

Amanda bent over further until she was leaning down inside the box.

"Why is this box so big?" she exclaimed, her voice echoing around her.

"It has to be big enough for all the books," said Dougie, very knowledgeably.

Amanda put her head up for a second and gave him a dirty look.

"That wasn't a real question. Look, Douglas, do you think you could help me here? We're running out of time! I'm looking for a book about goblins, and one about witches," she explained.

Dougie grunted and Amanda turned back to what she was doing, and grumbled, "They must be down the bottom somewhere."

"Oooh, here's one called *The Funny Ghost*… and one about a princess cat and… Oh, yuck! Here's one about scary animals."

"Oooh, can I see that?" Dougie leaned into the box too.

"Give me some room," said Amanda, elbowing him out of the way. She stretched as far as she could, grasping for some books she couldn't… quite… reach. Dougie stretched too, he wanted that scary animal book!

They were both leaning so far down into the box that their wiggling bottoms stuck up in the air, like a pair of diving pelicans. Then Dougie shouted, "There's the one about the goblins!"

"Where?" said Amanda, excitedly.

"Down there!" he pointed. "Are you blind?"

"I see it!" said Amanda, ignoring the last comment, and she reached out for the book at exactly the same time as Dougie did.

And... "WHAAAARRRRGGGGGGGHHHHHHHHH!" she screamed at the top of her lungs.

"WHAAARRGGGHHH!" Dougie yelled as well.

They were both FALLING.

Falling through air!

Falling in darkness!

They'd fallen into the library book box, and tumbled headfirst, feet-first, headfirst, until they lost all sense of direction and time.

CHAPTER 4

"WAAARRRGGGGHHHH," they both continued screaming…

and TWISTING…

and LOOPING

through the rushing, black air.

"WAAAARRRRGGGHHHHH!!!!!!!!" echoed back from the walls of the box.

Amanda flailed frantically, grabbing at the empty air around her for anything to hang onto. Now and again, she thumped against Dougie – knocking her elbow, knee, and then…

KA-THUMP!!! She hit the ground.

"OUCH!" she cried, and toppled sideways. She had landed on something really hard, and she sat with tears in her eyes and rubbed all the places that hurt. She was breathing heavily, her heartbeat thumped away in her ears, and her body was aching all over. For

a few more moments she sat there, then she heard
someone groaning beside her.

"Douglas? Is that you?" she panted.

"Yes," Dougie whimpered.

"Are you okay?"

"I'm sore," said Dougie. "Why did you pull my
hair?"

"I didn't touch your hair!"

"Well, something did, while we were falling!"

Amanda froze, wondering about that. Her pulse and breathing gradually slowed, and after a while she realised that she was sitting on something not just hard, but cold and hard... and wet. And it was absolutely silent around them. So silent that the silence was deafening.

Then...

PLOP!

"What was that?" she whispered.

PLOP! PLOP!

"It sounds like water dripping," Dougie whispered back. "It's so dark, I can't see anything... But it feels like we're in a cave."

"A cave? Ridiculous. It's probably a tunnel, or just some pipes under the library," said Amanda.

She squinted into the inky blackness. She couldn't see anything either. She felt the cold floor, and heard the water drip... drip... drip....

"Maybe it is a cave," she said and stood up before her bottom froze and stuck to the ground. "Whatever it is, we have to find our way out of here." Dougie grunted in agreement.

Amanda continued to stand there a bit dazed, and then she felt a soft, faint breeze on her face, that gave her goosebumps all over.

"Did you feel that?" she asked Dougie.

"Yes," he replied.

Amanda continued, "Remember our last school excursion? When we went down that cave? The guide told us that fresh air comes from openings in the rock. I'm sure it's the same with tunnels and pipes!"

"That's right!" said Dougie. "Maybe there's an opening that's big enough for us to climb out. But how do we find it? I can't see a thing."

"Trust me," said Amanda, beginning to feel adventurous. "Let's follow the direction of the breeze. Just grab hold of my hand so we can keep together."

"Do I have to?" asked Dougie.

"You're not going to get girl germs, Dougie. Come on! Give me your hand!" Amanda reached out and found Dougie's fingertips in the darkness. As she held his hand, she suddenly felt stronger.

"You've never called me Dougie before," Dougie said. "I like being called that."

"Don't go all mushy on me," said Amanda, squirming, and she started to walk into the breeze, leading him.

They slowly felt their way across the uneven floor. Their shoes slipped and slid on what felt like mud and wet rocks. Amanda steadied herself now and again with her free hand, resting it on cold, slimy walls. Once she almost fell, but got her balance just in time.

She paused a moment, her heart thumping, and then they walked on.

A little later, in the distance, they saw an opening. It looked like moonlight was shining through a hole, lighting the way.

"There's the exit!" said Dougie, and Amanda rolled her eyes.

"Obviously!" she replied.

And they moved quickly towards the light and more fresh air.

CHAPTER 5

They were standing outside, at the base of what seemed to be a huge hole in the ground, like a crater. Amanda looked back and saw that they hadn't been inside a man-made tunnel, but a cave, its entrance carved long ago into the rock by natural forces.

Moonlight streamed down, and as they looked around, Amanda and Dougie saw that they were totally surrounded by rocky cliffs rising high into the sky, and crowned at the top with tree canopies. Sparkling stars hung low, adorning the scene like flashing, brilliant jewels. The air was cool, and a heady perfume wafted from all the blossoms on the smaller trees growing at the base of the crater. They both breathed in deeply.

"Dougie, you can let go of my hand now," said Amanda.

"Oh!" Dougie dropped it quickly and said, "I told you it was a cave!!"

Amanda ignored him.

He continued, "Do you think this is an old volcano, or did a meteor land here?"

"I don't know," said Amanda, and she didn't really care. She was thinking.

"How are we going to get out of here?" asked Dougie.

"There must be a path somewhere. Can't you look?"

"Who says there's a path?" said Dougie, a little hurt.

"I say," said Amanda, grumpily.

"We could be the very first people in this place."

"Yeah, right."

"It's true. Like the first man on the moon – we could be the first ones here," insisted Dougie.

"Could not."

"Could so."

"Could not!"

"Could so..."

"COULD YOU BOTH PLEASE BE QUIET!" boomed a deep voice.

Amanda and Dougie both JUMPED! Their bickering stopped immediately.

"Who was that?" squeaked Amanda, chills snaking up her spine.

"I don't know!" Dougie squeaked back.

"JUST BE QUIET," boomed the voice again.

Amanda looked around.

"Can you see anyone?" she asked Dougie. He just shrugged his shoulders.

Then a strange humming sound started behind them.

Amanda turned and walked towards the *hum*, Dougie cautiously followed. As they got closer and closer to the sound, she realised that it was coming from a very old rock. She stopped in amazement, and something made her look up. Her jaw dropped to her ankles. The rock was big and tall, and in the shape of a huge lizard, a powerful lizard that was standing on strong hind legs and looking at them with bulging eyes.

"Well, what are you looking at?" asked the rock.

"Sorry," said Dougie, the first to speak. "We don't mean to be rude. We just haven't seen a humming… talking… rock lizard… before," he stammered.

"WHAT did you call me?" asked the rock.

"Shut up!" Amanda hissed, elbowing Dougie sharply in the ribs. She turned back and faced the rock. "I'm sorry, sir, we don't know your name."

"I am the Guardian of the Cave," said the rock.

"What are you guarding?" asked Dougie excitedly. "Buried treasure?"

The Guardian looked at him. "Yes. Treasure, of a sort," it replied.

"See, I told you people had been here!" Amanda said triumphantly, and she stuck out her tongue at Dougie.

"People have been here for tens of thousands of years, dear," noted the Guardian, dryly. Amanda felt silly.

"Where are they now?" asked Dougie.

"Well, they usually come here when it's hot and dry upstairs. Sometimes they'll visit on a special occasion but now the rains have come they won't be here for a while. Unless, of course, there's a special occasion," the Guardian added.

Amanda was thinking furiously fast and not paying any attention at all to what the Guardian said about the people and their special occasions. "What do you mean by *upstairs*?" she asked.

"Well," said the Guardian, "this is downstairs, and they live upstairs."

"Are you saying that there are stairs going up and out of here?" she said.

"Yes," mused the Guardian, "I suppose there are, but I can't see that well. If there are stairs, you should be able to see them when the sun comes up."

"Oh," said Amanda.

She thought for a moment, then Dougie asked, "How can you be a guard if you can't see that well?"

The Guardian of the Cave suddenly chuckled. "I *feel* what's happening. For example, there's no danger around tonight. Unless you have something planned!" It chuckled again and then said, "You both must be tired. You can sleep here at my feet if you like. You will be safe here. And I promise you the best Dreaming possible."

S-l-e-e-p.

Amanda hadn't thought about being tired at all, but just hearing that word triggered something in her brain, and she yawned at the same time as Dougie.

"Oh, I am sleepy," she said, and Dougie nodded his head drowsily in agreement.

They fell straight down onto the grass growing at the feet of the Guardian of the Cave, and were asleep before anything else was said.

CHAPTER 6

"Ahem."

Amanda stirred.

"AaaaaHEM."

Amanda sat bolt upright. The images of dancing people with dotted faces, clicking sticks and swirling, painted hands vanished instantly into her subconscious.

"Hello?" said a little voice near her ankles.

She looked down, and then rubbed her eyes violently.

"I'm sorry, did you say something?" she asked foolishly.

There was a little animal sitting in front of her. Since when could she hear animals speak?

"Excuse me!" exclaimed the furry little animal, jumping onto her lap and staring right into her face. "What are you doing down here?"

Dougie rolled over and yawned.

"What's going on? Can't you see I'm having the best dream?"

"Really! Well, I never!" the animal said with its uppity voice, and it jumped over and kicked him with its back paw. "I've got work to do here, and I can't do it if you're in the way!!"

Dougie didn't budge.

"Dougie! Wake up!" Amanda shook him by the shoulders. Dougie just grunted in reply. Amanda sighed and gave up. She looked at the creature again and asked curiously, "What are you?"

"WHAT am I? How rude you are!" said the animal, indignantly. "I am a numbat! TA-DAAAA!" And it struck a pose, as if it had just performed an amazing magical trick.

Amanda looked at it properly. It was a lovely-looking, sandy-red creature, with dark stripes on its back and a single stripe under each eye. *What a shame about the attitude*, she thought.

"I thought numbats were extinct," mumbled Dougie, who was finally getting his act together, groggily sitting up and apparently having no problem with the fact that Amanda was having a conversation with an animal.

"Well, that's the way you New People want it," snapped the numbat.

"What do you mean?" asked Amanda.

"Well, what do you New People do? We have a nice lifestyle here, and then you spoil it all by importing those ferocious foxes, with their big, sharp teeth and long, bushy tails. Not to mention the feral cats dumped here!" It continued without taking a breath. "They hiss and scratch and fur-fight all the time – not just with us, but also with one another! We're so tired of it all! Every night we're scared that we're going to be eaten! If they see us, they'll chase us. We spend half the night running and our days are shot to pieces!"

"Oh," said Amanda, suddenly feeling that she was witnessing a political speech. "That doesn't sound very good."

"Good? GOOD??! There's NOTHING good about it AT ALL!" yelled the numbat hysterically. "Except that I'm an excellent sprinter!" it sniffed. "There's nothing like being forced to run in order to stay alive! Anyway, you haven't answered my question. What are you doing down here?"

Amanda thought about it. How do you describe school library book boxes to a numbat? "Well, um… we got here by accident," she said.

"Well, we have to get you out of here now," said the numbat, looking at them suspiciously. "It gets very busy during the day and you're both in the way. Now, follow me."

Amanda and Dougie looked at each other and nodded, as the numbat turned and moved off. Amanda put her hand on the Guardian of the Cave and whispered quickly, "Goodbye Guardian. Thank you for the Dreams." It hummed something back, and she felt strange that she had felt compelled to do that, and a little sad at having to say goodbye. She turned and ran to catch up with Dougie and the numbat. They had already rounded the inside of the cliffs and appeared to be climbing a wall of stairs!

CHAPTER 7

The stairs were made of crumbling rocks, and were so steep you couldn't see an end to them. Amanda grew hot and sweaty as she climbed higher and higher it felt like she was walking into the sky. Her leg muscles ached.

Dougie and the numbat were just in front of her. The numbat stopped for a breath, so she and Dougie stopped as well, and took the opportunity to have a good look around.

Many beautiful birds were calling out amongst the trees. Kookaburras laughed crazily from the eucalypts, while some parrots with bright yellow rings around their necks darted and swooped between the branches, looking sideways at the strangers, as if unsure of whether or not to be afraid.

It was a hard climb, but the breeze was cool and the scent of peppermint was strong in the air. In a short time they were at the top of the rocky staircase.

Amanda turned and looked at the trees that now lay way below them. The crater was a huge expanse of twirled and twisted branches covered with red and yellow blossoms, interlaced with green-brown leaves. Looking more carefully through the trees she could just make out the lizard shape of the Guardian of the Cave, over on the far wall. The Guardian looked so small from here, but so wise, and seemed to be watching them. She shook her head – silly thoughts!

"Come on!" said the numbat, who was now in a bad temper from all the exercise. "This is no time for sightseeing! We have to get to the path, and then I have to go back down again before my visitors arrive. Nuisances!!" It took off down a different track and Amanda and Dougie followed, hurrying to keep up. They went beneath trees, around trees, even through big, burnt-out hollow trees. Bees hummed past their heads, and some honeyeaters flew crazily above, chattering amongst themselves or chasing one another. They paused for breath next to a tree that had red gum running down its outside, like blood running from a sore.

"That's why they're called gum trees – they bleed like the gums in your mouth after you've lost a tooth," said Dougie.

"Oh, you're such a scientist!" replied Amanda, not knowing whether or not to believe him.

"Here we are!" interrupted the numbat, stopping what could have been a very good argument. "Follow this path as far as it goes, and a friend of mine will come to help you."

"How will your friend know we're coming?" asked Dougie.

The numbat snorted derisively, "Haven't you heard of the Bush Telegraph?"

It turned and scurried off, muttering under its breath, "Nuisances!"

"Wait!" called out Amanda. "How far do we have to go?"

But the numbat had already disappeared.

"What an unusual creature," said Dougie.

"It could say the same thing about you," said Amanda.

Dougie looked at her.

"We forgot to say thanks, too!" Amanda sighed, and then started along the path they'd been shown.

CHAPTER 8

Amanda was still walking ahead of Dougie. She felt a little grumpy, and wanted the space to think. She was very excited by what had happened so far, and she wondered what would happen next.

Lost in her own thoughts, she envisaged the school library, the cave, the talking rock and the yabbering numbat. She was swept along in this whirlpool of images and forgot all about Dougie, until he called out, "My feet are sore. How long have we been walking?"

"It's only been about half an hour," said Amanda, and she stopped and waited for him.

"How much further do we have to go?" he grumbled, as he hobbled closer.

"I don't know, but have you noticed anything?" said Amanda.

"Yeah, my feet hurt," said Dougie, bending over to look at his shoes.

"Apart from your feet, Dougie."

Dougie hadn't thought of anything, except his feet for ages, and said nothing.

"Dougie, you're the one that reads all the science books! We've been going downhill for quite a while now, there are fewer trees, more shrubs, and it's getting cooler..."

Dougie looked at her like he didn't care.

Amanda, although angry, made her voice lighter.

"Can you smell anything in the air?" she asked patiently.

Dougie sniffed loudly, like he was drawing up snot for a good spitball.

How gross, thought Amanda.

"I smell salt," Dougie said.

"Exactly! I think we're near the ocean."

"I can't see any ocean. I'm hungry."

"Dougie, just stop whining. Isn't this great?"

Dougie said nothing.

"Dougie?"

"When are we going home?" he sniffed again, this time a delicate hanky sniff.

Aren't boys supposed to be strong? Amanda thought, pretending not to notice.

She sighed.

"Look, I don't know where we're going. I don't even know how to get back to the cave, let alone the school library. We'll just have to keep on walking until we can find someone to help us. The numbat said that a friend would come and help, remember?"

Dougie kept on looking at his feet. He was trying not to cry. Inwardly, Amanda knew exactly how he felt, but she wasn't going to show it. She tried again. "Dougie, do you remember in the library when you told me that you liked real adventure stories, because you'd never end up in space, or fighting dragons?"

Dougie looked up. "Yes."

"Well, think of this as our first real adventure, with tunnels and caves and rock lizards and numbats and…" she stopped.

"Yes. It is an adventure, isn't it?" Dougie said, a hint of a smile on his face. Then he looked at Amanda with brighter eyes, as if she'd really helped him.

She smiled back, encouragingly. "Well, that's the way to look at it! Don't worry. You're not on your own. I'm here too, remember? It's a shared adventure. But," she admitted, "I need your help with all the stuff you might know."

"Oh," said Dougie. "Well, I've read a lot of survival books, too."

"Then we're going to be all right."

Amanda felt a lot better. The fear in her own stomach – the fear of the unknown – turned back into a thrill of excitement! Who knew what would happen next?

CHAPTER 9

Grey sand turned to red dirt, the path gradually widened, and the trees became sparser. Finally, Amanda and Dougie found themselves standing at the top of a hill. Down below, directly west, lay a line of trees, beyond which the bluest ocean Amanda had ever seen glinted in the sunlight. Clouds drifted aimlessly above as if they were also waiting for directions. Farmland stretched for miles and miles to the north and south, with the fields on either side filled with long grass. A few native trees were strewn here and there, creating pockets of shade. The sound of bleating sheep came in the distance.

Amanda held in her breath as she looked around.

"Wow," she said, finally breathing out. She felt tears in her eyes.

It was such a beautiful place, and for a few minutes they both stood there, and silently taking it all in.

Then Amanda heard something move behind her, and she turned and glimpsed a flash of gold.

Dougie said, "Look! There are the sheep! Maybe we'll see a farmer."

Amanda immediately forgot what she'd seen, and strained her eyes, searching the landscape. "I can't see any farmers. Or any houses," she said. "Shall we keep on walking?"

"I think so," said Dougie. "It's so hot."

He smiled. "Hey, we could go for a swim in the ocean! Then I can soak my feet in the salt water!" He was really beginning to cheer up.

"Good idea!" said Amanda, smiling back at him. "Let's go straight down. The path continues over there."

"Maybe there'll be some fresh water as well," said Dougie, and he pointed. "Look at all the trees growing over there – they have to be drinking something!"

They both walked steadily down the sloping path and into a small grove of trees at the base of the hill. The leaves whispered secrets softly above them as they made their way along the narrow, clear-cut track. After a few minutes they heard the sound of trickling water and without saying a word, moved quickly towards it.

Dougie went ahead, climbing carefully over grey rocks covered with pale green lichen. A few metres further on, they came across a small rock pool, shaded by paperbark trees.

"Look at this!" smiled Amanda. She moved over to the water, squatted down, and took a long drink. She gasped as the cold liquid slid down the inside of her throat. When she finished she moved back from the water's edge and rested against the papery trunk of the tree closest to her. The bark rustled comfortably beneath her back.

Dougie was drinking as much as he could too. He gulped and gulped, then finally stood up and shivered. "It's so cold!" he said through chattering teeth.

"Yeah," Amanda yawned in agreement, "too cold to swim here."

"I think so too. Let's go and swim down at the beach!"

"Can we just rest a second?" asked Amanda. She was quite comfortable where she was.

"Okay."

Amanda now leant her full weight onto the trunk of the tree, and shut her eyes. A moment later she thought she heard something move, and half-opened her eyes. Through her eyelashes she saw something golden waved at her!

She stood up, alert. "Dougie! Did you see that?"

"See what?" asked Dougie, who was sunning himself like a snake on a warm rock.

"Shhh!! Over there!"

Dougie looked hard, but couldn't see anything.

"You must be hallucinating," he teased her.

"I am not!" pouted Amanda. Then she looked again. Where had that thing gone? "Oh well," she laughed, "maybe you're right. We haven't eaten for ages after all. Let's get going."

They both got up lazily and picked their way back to the path, then continued walking towards the ocean.

CHAPTER 10

It took no time at all to walk from the rock pool down to the beach. The sound of the waves gradually got louder and louder, and the path became so sandy it was difficult to walk on. Amanda felt as if her feet were in a pot of glue, so she lifted them higher with each step. That's when she discovered that the sand squeaked under her feet. She giggled, and so did Dougie. It sounded as if the sand was talking to them, so they jumped around and made a conversation of squeaky sand sounds. Before they knew it, they were standing on the beach before a small bay.

The bay was the shape of a cupped hand, with the wrist part being a long, solid piece of rock that created a corner to their right, and craggy rocks in the shape of nimble, old fingers pointing off somewhere, to their left.

"I'm going in for a swim!" yelled Dougie.

He threw off his shoes and socks, and then the rest of his clothes!

"Dougie! How could you?!" Amanda squeezed her eyes shut and made herself busy with her shoelaces. She didn't see *anything*, she was laughing so hard.

Dougie ran full pelt into the water.

"Watch out for seaweed… and things that bite," Amanda sang out. She then left her shoes lying in the sand and walked down the beach.

There were so many different things to look at – periwinkles on the shore, mussels clinging to the rocks, and tiny holes in the sand that shellfish might be breathing through. *Maybe some baby crabs are hiding down there too*, she thought.

The wet sand slipped and oozed between her toes, and as she scrunched along, she felt as if her feet were being massaged by every single grain. She reached the end of the small bay, and looked at the craggy rocks in front of her. They looked too sharp to climb, so she turned back.

In the distance she saw that Dougie was still having a wild time in the water, splashing about as if he hadn't had a bath in a month. He probably hadn't. Amanda giggled. He looked like a crazy duck.

Then she slowly retraced her footsteps until she got back to her shoes, and then continued walking in the other direction.

This time she could walk across the rock at the end of the bay, because it was long and smooth, and had been rounded by the tide. The sun was getting hotter. Usually she would have her favourite pink straw hat on her head. If Mum had been here, she'd be carrying Amanda's hat for her. *But Mum isn't here*, Amanda thought, and got a little teary.

She sat down on the rock, and shielded her eyes as best she could from the sun. Her feet dangled over the edge, almost touching the small waves that noisily lapped against the rock.

She peered through the clear, crystal water, and felt sad. But then, as her eyes adjusted to the sunlight, she realised that she could see the ocean floor, and some baby fish swimming around.

She smiled and relaxed a little.

The sunlight, and the sound of the waves made her feel dozy again, and just as she was about to fall asleep, someone behind her said, "Hello."

Amanda turned, and looked over her shoulder. There was a golden flash! She blinked.

"Hello?" came the voice a little more strongly, but over her other shoulder.

Surprised, Amanda turned the other way, and found herself saying "Hello" back, to the most beautiful grey kangaroo.

"You really should be out of the sun. It's getting pretty hot," the kangaroo said, fluttering its long eyelashes at her.

"I suppose you're right." Amanda was confused. Was she in a dream?

Nevertheless, she stood up and walked wonkily to the trees that lined the beach. The kangaroo hopped right behind her, and when they both reached the closest tree, they slumped down in its shade.

Dougie was still mucking around in the water, but seemed to be slowing down.

"Numbat told me you'd be here," said the kangaroo. "I'm sorry I'm late, I made an emergency detour because I saw a fox and went to warn my friends."

"Oh. I'm sorry," said Amanda, sympathetically. "Can't they be stopped?"

"Yes," said the kangaroo. "The New People are putting down poison and traps. But some of the traps have killed my friends, too. There's no easy solution."

Amanda didn't know what to say.

She suddenly realised that some people, well, animals, had more dangerous days than she did. Then, for some reason, Big Mel leapt into her mind. Big Mel twisting her arm. She couldn't imagine what it would be like to be chased every day by her!

"School's a bit like that," she said to the kangaroo. She hadn't thought about school for such a long time.

"What? They poison and trap you, too?"

Amanda laughed. "Sometimes the canteen food tastes like poison, but it isn't... And sometimes school feels like a big trap, a trap for kids. We're all stuck there. And we're all so different, but we're trying to be the same – trying to be liked, trying to fit in..."

Her voice trailed off, but the kangaroo was listening carefully, so she continued, "And the awful thing is… I don't fit in. I go to school every day, and I know that I'll like class. I like learning new things. But then there's a long lunch break. We've got time to do things, but no-one talks to me, or wants to play with me. So I go to the library."

"Don't you have *any* friends?" asked the kangaroo, as diplomatically as it could.

"Well, I do now," said Amanda, pointing at Dougie, who was just about to get out of the water. "And I have had girl friends at school, but sometimes they act like they're your best friend, and then the next day they've decided you're not their friend anymore. And you don't know why. It happens a lot." She gulped.

The kangaroo thought for a while. "That sounds really hard. I have a lot of friends. But the thing about friends is – some of them you've known since they were born, some move to other places, and some aren't really your friends.

"I had a kookaburra friend who was okay in the beginning, but then she started to laugh at me, whatever I did, especially when I was learning how to hop.

"The other kookaburras sat and watched quietly. But this particular friend kept on saying that I was stupid, in front of everybody! I then realised that *this* kookaburra wasn't being a friend at all!

"The funny thing was, it would have been very easy for the other kookaburras to join in and laugh as well, but they didn't. They were all the same type of bird, but had very different characters."

Amanda thought about Big Mel and her troll friends, all laughing at her. "What do you do, when it's more than one person laughing at you?" she asked the kangaroo.

"Just remember who you are and don't listen to them," the kangaroo replied. "They're only strong when they're together. They're probably all just trying to be liked by the others in the group and become mean. So you just be yourself. Be who you truly are, and you'll feel strong."

"How do I know who I am?" asked Amanda.

Just then Dougie came racing up to the tree with half his clothes on.

"HELLO!" he shouted at the kangaroo, as he struggled to put on his shirt.

The kangaroo's ears twitched in alarm.

"Hello," it replied politely, and then it turned back to Amanda and said, "One day you'll have a true friend – someone who'll be your friend no matter what. I promise… I have to go now."

The kangaroo looked at Dougie, "Nice meeting you, friend."

Then it hopped along the beach and just as it got to the edge of the bush it turned and called out, "I almost forgot. Go around to the left of the beach, and keep your eyes peeled for the boat! Goodbye!" Then it faded into the trees.

"What boat?" Dougie flopped down on the sand and started putting on his shoes.

"I don't know," said Amanda.

"That was the best swim I've had in ages," continued Dougie, not listening to her. "The water's so clear. You can see the ocean floor! Amanda, are you listening to me?"

"What?" Amanda said distractedly – she was trying to remember everything the kangaroo had said to her.

"What did the kangaroo mean about a boat?" Dougie said again.

"Boat? I don't know," said Amanda.

They both sat there on the sand for a while, looking out to sea, adrift in their own thoughts.

CHAPTER 11

After her short rest, Amanda was ready to move again, even though she was feeling tired and VERY hungry. She was also starting to worry about *everything*.

"Come on, Dougie," she said, in a wobbly voice.

Dougie rubbed his eyes. "What are we going to do now?" he said. "How are we going to get back to school? When are we going to eat? What time is it?"

"Stop asking questions, Dougie!" she yelled, and then promptly burst into tears. Dougie looked about him like he didn't know what to say.

"Sorry," he said.

"No, I'm sorry." Amanda's voice trembled. "I just don't know what to do. I'm sorry I yelled at you."

"Well," said Dougie, "I think we should walk around the corner of the bay, like the kangaroo said."

"I was going to check it out before, but the rocks are pretty sharp," said Amanda.

"You'll have shoes on this time," said Dougie, "plus we can help each other. It should be easier with the two of us."

"Okay," she said.

She stood up and dusted the sand off her clothes, and they walked towards the rocky end of the beach.

The sky darkened as Amanda and Dougie made their way over the spiky rocks. Sometimes she grabbed his hand, and sometimes he grabbed hers. It was nice to have that little feeling of safety, and she also felt encouraged. Maybe they could make it around the bend!

When they did get around the corner, there was another bay covered with the same sharp rocks, but this time with no soft sand to be seen anywhere. Rocks covered everything.

Amanda bit her lip, and cried out, "Oh, no! What are we going to do now?"

She dropped to the ground and started to cry.

Dougie didn't move.

"Ahoy there!"

Amanda didn't look up.

"AHOY!"

53

"Look!" said Dougie, pointing. "It's a fisherman!"

An old wooden boat was coming towards them, with a fisherman sitting amongst some empty crates. He was rowing with strong, broad strokes.

The boat got closer and closer, and they both realised that it wasn't a fisherman at all; it was a fisherwoman, with a face so old and wrinkly it was like looking at a map.

The boat glided up to them, then turned so it was parallel to the rocks.

The fisherwoman looked up at them and smiled. She had the crookedest, yellowest teeth they had ever seen. "What are you two scallywags up to?" she asked kindly, in a raspy voice.

"We're lost," said Dougie.

"Have you run away?"

"No, not exactly," said Amanda.

She looked at them. "Kanga told me you'd be here. Get into the boat, and I'll take you to the sand dune. From there, you'll be able to find your way back to school."

Neither of the children moved. How did she know where their school was?

"What's wrong?" the fisherwoman asked.

Dougie mumbled, "You're a stranger. We shouldn't go anywhere with strangers."

She roared with laughter.

"Douglas Dunkin and Amanda Annanda, I know exactly who you are," she said. Then she calmed down and introduced herself.

"I'm Mrs Crabapple. Come on," she said, "grab hold of my arm, and I'll help you both onto the boat." She stretched out an arm as gnarled as a tree branch.

Amanda was astounded that Mrs Crabapple knew who they were and got onto the boat after Dougie, tightly holding the old lady's arm as she climbed aboard.

There was just enough space between the crab nets and crates for all of them to sit, and the boat stank a bit of fish guts, but it was nice to have someone looking after them, so Amanda didn't mind too much. She sat quietly and tried not to wrinkle her nose.

"Are you hungry?" asked Mrs Crabapple.

"Starving!" said Dougie, who'd been holding his breath, trying not to inhale the putrid air. He breathed in again loudly, then when he saw Amanda glaring at him, he released the air like a blowfish.

"Reach into that hessian bag," Mrs Crabapple said, not noticing anything they were up to, "and you'll find some apples. Then when we get to the sand dune we can all have some bread and cheese, as well."

"Thanks," said Amanda, smiling at the old lady and taking an apple out of the bag. She munched away and thought that this was the best tasting apple she'd ever eaten. But maybe that was because she was starving.

Mrs Crabapple started rowing, and the boat moved slowly back out to sea. The tide was coming in, so they drifted easily around the next corner. The rocking motion made Amanda feel very sleepy again, and she started to drift away. Mrs Crabapple smiled down at both of them and let them fall asleep.

A little while later Amanda opened her eyes. She looked over at Mrs Crabapple, who gave her a wink, and then pointed to something behind Amanda's shoulder. Amanda turned and her eyes widened.

In front of the boat was the biggest cave she had ever seen. The cave was right on the edge of the water, and its mouth was so wide it was the size of a whale's yawn.

"Dougie, look at this!" Amanda squealed.

Dougie sat up straight away, shook his head, blinked, and then turned to where she was pointing.

"Oh, boy! What a massive cave!" he said.

There were hundreds of stalagmites and stalactites inside. They pointed up from the floor and down from the ceiling, glistening in the half-light.

Cool air blew across the boat.

"Just like having ants in your pants – the mites go up and the tights come down," recited Mrs Crabapple.

Amanda and Dougie looked at her strangely.

"Stalagmites – mites go up, stalactites – tights come down," Mrs Crabapple said with a grin. "That's how you remember their directions."

The penny dropped, and Dougie laughed so hard he almost fell out of the boat. Amanda wasn't sure if he was overdoing it.

"Is this the cave we were in?" she asked, looking pointedly at him.

"I don't think so," he replied quite normally.

Mrs Crabapple looked at both of them.

"You were in another cave?" she asked.

"Yes," said Amanda, "the one with the Guardian of the Cave – he looks like a big lizard, and you climb a rocky staircase to get out."

"Well, well, well, three holes in the ground," murmured Mrs Crabapple, "you have come a long way. Let's get going. We should be at the sand dune within the hour."

She picked up the oars again and rowed past the mouth of the cave. Dougie was entranced by it, but finally settled down again. Amanda rested her head on his shoulder, because it was more comfortable. So comfortable that she'd soon fallen asleep again.

CHAPTER 12

"Here we are, kiddies."

Amanda and Dougie sat up, and looked about. There in front of the boat was a huge sand dune that swept up into the sky in the shape of a giant wave. As Amanda looked at the top of the dune, she noticed that the sun was trying to peep out from between the clouds. Some rays of light fell gently around them. It felt like it was late afternoon, already.

Mrs Crabapple anchored the boat close to shore. They all ate some bread and cheese together, and drank some water from an antique water bottle Dougie found near his feet. Then Mrs Crabapple gave them some instructions.

"Climb to the top of the sand dune and start walking directly away from the ocean," she said. "You'll find a pathway there between the trees. Keep your eyes open for black snakes – they're called dugites –

and follow the path until you come to an open area where the shrubs are very low to the ground and the wildflowers grow. You'll be picked up there."

"Could you just go back to the bit about the snakes?" said Amanda, worried.

"Leave them alone, and they'll leave you alone," Mrs Crabapple advised. "I really don't think you'll see any – they've most likely finished their sunbaking for the day, but if you do come across one, slowly back away from it so it won't be scared. Snakes only attack when they're scared. Just like people."

"Do snakes get scared?" asked Dougie.

"You betcha!" grinned Mrs Crabapple, with her toothy smile. "Anyway, you'd both best be off. I don't want you to be late."

"Thank you, Mrs. Crabapple," Amanda and Dougie chorused.

Then they jumped off the bow of the boat into the water. Their shoes got a bit wet, but it was nice and cooling for their feet.

Once on shore, Amanda turned and waved back to Mrs. Crabapple who had already started rowing.

"Take care, kiddies." Her voice floated across the water, and then she was gone from sight.

CHAPTER 13

"Well, we've eaten and rested. I'm feeling quite good. How about you Dougie?" asked Amanda.

Dougie turned and pouted, "I wish we could have gone inside that cave! Imagine if there were bats in there!"

"Well we can't see everything, or we'd never get back to school," Amanda said.

School.

They looked at each other.

"It's getting late. We should start climbing this sand dune."

Dougie nodded. "I'll go first," he said, and he started to climb.

It took ages. For every two steps forward, Amanda seemed to slide one step back. It was quite impossible. Then the wind came up and blew sand all over her and into her eyes. She started to feel dizzy

and stopped to check to see how far they'd come.
It made her stomach flip somersaults to look so far
down, but at least they were making progress.

She sighed, and turned, and started climbing
again. After stopping for a few rests she noticed that
Dougie was getting further and further ahead. He was
soon far away, so she cried out, "Hey! Wait for me!"

But Dougie didn't hear her and then he
disappeared over the top of the dune.

Amanda was distraught.

"DOUGIE!!!!"

But it was all in vain. There was no Dougie.

She crumpled onto the sand, sliding down the slope a little, and burst into tears.

She cried for a little while, and then all of a sudden, felt some sunlight gently touch her on the shoulder.

"Are you okay?" asked a soft voice.

She twisted her tear-stained face around but couldn't see anyone. *Why is this happening again?* she wondered.

"I'm here," said the voice.

She looked around again, and as her tears dried and her vision came back into focus she saw a golden shape standing in front of her. It was a small girl, whose whole body was the colour of light gold!

"Hello?" Amanda said, not believing her eyes. "Who are you?"

"Who do you think I am?" the girl giggled.

"I don't know... but I feel like I know you," said Amanda.

"Well you do," said the girl, smiling.

This is weird, thought Amanda. Then a strange, powerful feeling swept over her. Her eyes boggled with what she saw. She was so scared she held her breath, and then shut her eyes as tightly as she could. The feeling didn't go away with her eyes shut, but got stronger and stronger. Her eyelids felt like they were being prised open, so she stopped trying to keep them shut, and on opening them, saw that the golden girl was growing. She was getting taller and taller, and stretching wider and wider, and just as Amanda was about to scream she realised she was looking at herself.

CHAPTER 14

HERSELF??!!

Amanda couldn't believe it.

Then the golden girl smiled at her, and she immediately smiled back. Suddenly all her fears disappeared, and she felt really alive. And happy. And safe. All at the same time!

"What... Who... Why are you here?" she asked, tremulously.

"I'm always with you," said the girl.

"What do you mean?" asked Amanda.

"Well, I'm here to tell you that I'm always here. Weren't you looking for Your Self?" asked the girl.

Amanda looked at her mirror image and the girl's face suddenly dissolved before her eyes, and she saw herself back down in the bay talking to the kangaroo. "How do I know who I am?" Amanda heard herself ask.

Then the girl's face was before her once more, and Amanda looked at her.

The girl continued, "You asked the question – one of the most important questions of your life. And I'm here to remind you that you *know* who you are."

Amanda looked at her, "Did I see you earlier today?"

"Yes. I had to wait for the right time to talk to you. The right time is when you're alone," said the girl, "when you can hear your own voice clearly."

Amanda blinked.

"So many unexpected things can happen in life," said the girl, "and sometimes they happen all at once. It can be very confusing. Like the times when you feel that your parents don't care about what you do; or that your teachers are putting you down with your latest test score; or your friends like you one day, then they say they hate you; or you get teased about your name; or you get your arm twisted. It all gets a bit much doesn't it?"

Amanda suddenly felt sad, because the girl was talking about things that she hadn't told anyone. She looked at her, and saw her own tears reflected in the girl's eyes.

"Don't get upset," smiled the girl, "I'm the *real* you, I'm always with you, and I'm here to help you."

She paused and then said, "Do you remember the last time you were feeling bad at school?"

Amanda nodded, "Yes."

"Remember when she grabbed your arm – what did you want to do?" asked the girl.

"I wanted to hurt her back!" said Amanda.

"And?"

"And make her feel like crying, too. Especially when her friends started laughing at me."

"But what did you do?" asked the girl.

"Nothing," Amanda sniffed, "because I'm not as strong as her."

The girl said gently, "You are strong, but maybe not physically. When someone treats you badly, it shows how weak they are. People such as Big Mel like to hurt others because they don't feel good about themselves. The more Big Mel hurts others, the more she hurts *Her* Self."

"I don't understand," said Amanda.

"You'll understand as you grow," said the girl, then she stopped talking and waited.

Amanda thought for a moment, and then she confessed.

"Sometimes I feel like giving up," she said. "Giving up on school, my family, myself... but there's always a little voice that speaks to me inside my head, and it makes me feel good. It says that I shouldn't worry, that I shouldn't give up, and that I'll feel better about things tomorrow. Is that you?"

The girl smiled and said, "Yes, because I am everything that is good about you. *Everything that is Good.*"

Amanda felt like crying. It dawned on her that she really had found herself.

The girl smiled even more gently at her. "I don't have much time, so listen carefully. Anytime that you're feeling upset, or a little lost, just find a quiet place to calm down. Breathe slowly. Breathe in all the good around you, and breathe out all your fears. Every time you do this you'll feel Your Self again. Because it doesn't matter what people say about you, or how they hurt you – it's all about how you *feel* about Your Self. Think of all the good things you've learned from your Mum and Dad, and your teachers at school that have taught you how to be Your Self and how to think for Your Self. Also, think about what you've learned from all your friends – those past and present."

Amanda immediately thought about Dougie and wondered where he was.

"He's at the top waiting for you," said the girl, "and he's thinking about climbing down to help you."

They smiled at each other.

"One last thing," the girl continued, "I know that you feel like giving up right now, and that it is easier to get help from Dougie. But how about you try to get to the top by yourself? There are times in your life where you have to ask for someone else's help, and that's all right, but for these sorts of things, do it yourself - because you'll always learn something. Including knowing that you CAN do anything you put your mind to!"

"AMANDA!!" Dougie shouted from above.

"Be the best you can be, Amanda," the girl said quickly. "Be kind. Be a good friend to others. Be honest. Do this and when the bad times come, and you really do need other people's help, they'll be there for you, because they'll know who you really are, and what you stand for in this life."

"Amanda!" It was Dougie's voice again.

Amanda tried to remember all the things being said. It felt so important to remember – like it was the most important lesson of her life. It was like she had touched a deep place in her own heart.

She blinked, and the girl vanished.

"Amanda!" she cried out to Her Self.

Silence. Full, happy, loving silence.

"AMANDA? Are you all right?" Dougie was yelling from the top of the dune.

She looked up at him, "I'm all right! I was just… thinking. I'll be up there in a second."

His laughter filtered down. "I think it will take you longer than that! I'll just wait here. Oh, I've found the path!"

Amanda gathered all her strength together, got up and clambered up the slope on all fours.

She could do this.

She could do this by herself.

She whispered into the air, "Thank you, I'll never forget this."

Her whole body was glowing, and she smiled and picked up speed.

CHAPTER 15

Amanda and Dougie sat at the top of the dune. Dougie was still waiting for Amanda to get her breath back. It was such a hard climb, but she had made it!

The view itself was breathtaking, and she looked back down at the never-ending ocean, the rocks, and the swirling sand.

"Ready to go again?" said Dougie.

"Yes. I wish we had some water."

"Well, it shouldn't be too far now," he said, "the path is over there." He pointed towards a couple of trees.

They both stood up and went to the pathway. It was bordered by tall, thick shrubs. Some of the shrubs were flowering heavily, and as Amanda and Dougie walked, bees whizzed past their ears, buzzing aggressively. They were very different to the humming bees they'd seen in the morning.

"Be careful!" Dougie called out each time he dodged one.

Amanda remembered her Dad being stung by a bee on the foot once. It hadn't been very funny, but she giggled as she remembered him hopping around on one leg all over the lawn at home, saying, "Shucks! Shucks! Aw, shucks!" She still didn't know what 'shucks' meant. Mind you, it would have been a different story if Dad had been allergic to bees. She stopped laughing.

The shrubs became shorter and shorter, and soon they were surrounded by small nameless birds that flitted erratically over a field of wildflowers. There were eggs and bacon, donkey orchids, and beautiful kangaroo paws. The sun was fading in the sky, and it was starting to get very cool. Just then a loud sound came from above their heads.

"Look at that!" Dougie cried out.

A HUGE bird was flying above them in circles. It seemed to stop in the air when it heard Dougie's voice, and it looked directly at them.

And then it dropped.

A HUGE screech filled the air.

The bird was aiming for them!

"IT'S AN EAGLE!!!!!!!" Dougie screamed.

The eagle dive-bombed them. Amanda screamed out and covered her head with her arms.

"Pheeeeeeeuuuuuu," screeched the eagle, as it sped around for a second attack.

This time there was a huge THWACK!!!!

"AAAAAARRRRRGGGGGHHHHHHHH!!!!!!!!!!!"

Amanda and Dougie screamed at the top of their lungs.

"Oooomph," went the eagle, as it struggled back into the sky, its talons fastened tightly onto their clothes. It flapped its wings in huge, wave-like motions, trying to get airborne.

"Aaaaaarrrrggggggghhh!!!" Amanda screamed more quietly, with her eyes shut.

Then, she was silent, and a certain giddiness overcame her.

She opened her eyes, and couldn't believe what she saw.

The bird was above them, and moving higher and higher into the sky. Amanda realised that she and Dougie were dangling beneath its body, and they had the most amazing view below them.

There was the ocean on the left, farmland on the right, and bush directly below.

Far in the distance to the north, was a big, black hole in the ground. It looked like the crater.

It was such a glorious sight, even if she had had any breath left, Amanda still wouldn't know what to say.

She couldn't believe how beautiful, and how different, each part of the land was. How beautiful and different the trees and plants and animals were. *Just like people*, Amanda thought.

The eagle changed direction, and so did Amanda's thoughts.

She thought of all the animals she'd met that day, and all the animals she still wanted to meet in her lifetime. She thought about kind Mrs Crabapple, and the Guardian of the Cave.

The eagle turned again, and there in the clutch of the eagle's claws Amanda felt excited about her future, and all the things that she could study and work towards, and what she could do for the environment, and what she could do for people. She thought of everyone who loved her or cared about her. She thought of all the things she could give back in return for all the gifts she'd received. She thought…

BANG!!!!

A huge sound exploded in her ears.

CHAPTER 16

"WHAT ON EARTH DO YOU TWO THINK YOU'RE DOING???!!!!"

Amanda's mind exploded, along with the vision of the countryside.

"Ooomph!" She'd been hurled to her feet, and landed on some carpet. Dougie was sitting next to her.

"WELL? What on earth were you doing, jumping into that library book box?"

It was Mrs Pritchard, and she had her hands knotted onto the backs of their shirts. Amanda was speechless.

"Well, who's going to tell me?" Mrs Pritchard snarled. Then she let go of both of them, and grabbed Amanda's shoulders, swung her around and eyeballed her with her yellow eyes.

"You said that you were going to look for those library books," she hissed.

Amanda was still in shock. What had just happened?

"Do you mean these books, Mrs. Pritchard?" asked Dougie, with the sweetest smile he could manage with both his knees knocking. He handed her the goblin book and witch book that Amanda had returned that morning. Amanda stared at him, and he winked at her.

"Well," sniffed Mrs Pritchard, "thank you, Douglas Dunkin. As for you, Missy," she looked at Amanda again, "the lunch bell has just rung, so it's too late for you to borrow any books today! Now, both of you, GET TO CLASS!!"

Amanda opened her mouth to say something, but Dougie grabbed her by the arm and dragged her outside the library door, calling out, "Thanks Mrs Pritchard!"

They ran towards their classrooms.

"Dougie," said Amanda shakily.

"Yep?" he said, grinning at her.

"Um, did... did that... were we... cave, boat..."

"Yes!" Dougie cried. "Wasn't it wicked! Look at our shoes!"

Amanda looked down and saw that her shoes were wet and covered in sand. She laughed. "So it did happen!"

"You betcha! Let's get to class now. We can talk about it after school."

Amanda nodded. She was so happy. She felt transformed. She knew now that the world was a bigger place than she could see. She knew that this country had a past that she didn't know or understand, yet. She knew that the plants and animals had to be protected. And she knew that help could come from the strangest of places.

She also realised for the first time that she WAS strong on the inside, and that from now on she would strive to be her True Self – to be the best person she was able to be, the best person she was born to be.

Meanwhile, back in the library, Mrs Pritchard was scowling down at the floor, and shaking her head incredulously.

There, in front of the library book box, was a pile of sand and wet shoeprints.

About the Author

Alison has a background in music, acting, musical theatre, writing, and teaching. She has lived in Australia, Japan, and Singapore, travelled extensively and has learned from many spiritual teachers, as well as through her own personal experience, that the world we live in is magic! She teaches piano, meditation, and conducts energy healing sessions for children and adults in Singapore and Australia. She strongly believes that we all need to connect with nature in order to connect more deeply with our "True Selves", our highest potential, and from that understanding do our work in a more creative manner. She is the founder of Meditation~Creation.

www.ingramcontent.com/pod-product-compliance
Lightning Source LLC
Chambersburg PA
CBHW070350130626
46556CB00007B/3108